A Note to Parents and Caregivers:

Read-it! Readers are for children who are just starting on the amazing road to reading. These beautiful books support both the acquisition of reading skills and the love of books.

 The PURPLE LEVEL presents basic topics and objects using high frequency words and simple language patterns.

 The RED LEVEL presents familiar topics using common words and repeating sentence patterns.

 The BLUE LEVEL presents new ideas using a larger vocabulary and varied sentence structure.

 The YELLOW LEVEL presents more challenging ideas, a broad vocabulary, and wide variety in sentence structure.

 The GREEN LEVEL presents more complex ideas, an extended vocabulary range, and expanded language structures.

 The ORANGE LEVEL presents a wide range of ideas and concepts using challenging vocabulary and complex language structures.

When sharing a book with your child, read in short stretches, pausing often to talk about the pictures. Have your child turn the pages and point to the pictures and familiar words. And be sure to reread favorite stories or parts of stories.

There is no right or wrong way to share books with children. Find time to read with your child, and pass on the legacy of literacy.

Adria F. Klein, Ph.D.
Professor Emeritus
California State University
San Bernardino, California

Editor: Patricia Stockland
Page Production: Melissa Kes/JoAnne Nelson/Tracy Davies
Art Director: Keith Griffin
Managing Editor: Catherine Neitge
The illustrations in this book were done in watercolor.

Picture Window Books
151 Good Counsel Drive
P.O. Box 669
Mankato, MN 56002-0669
877-845-8392
www.picturewindowbooks.com

Printed in the United States of America in North Mankato, Minnesota.
012010
005656

Library of Congress Cataloging-in-Publication Data
Jones, Christianne C.
The little red hen / by Christianne C. Jones ; illustrated by Natalie Magnuson.
p. cm. — (Read-it! readers folk tales)
Summary: The little red hen finds none of the lazy barnyard animals willing to help
her plant, harvest, or grind wheat into flour, but all are eager to eat the bread she
makes from it.
ISBN 978-1-4048-0975-8 (hardcover)
ISBN 978-1-4048-2170-5 (paperback)
ISBN 978-1-4048-5957-9 (paperback)
[1. Folklore.] I. Magnuson, Natalie, ill. II. Title. III. Series: Read-it! readers
folk tales.
PZ8.1.J646Li 2004
398.24'528625—dc22
2004018439

The Little Red Hen

By Christianne C. Jones

Illustrated by Natalie Magnuson

Special thanks to our advisers for their expertise:

Adria F. Klein, Ph.D.
Professor Emeritus, California State University
San Bernardino, California

Susan Kesselring, M.A.
Literacy Educator
Rosemount-Apple Valley-Eagan (Minnesota) School District

PICTURE WINDOW BOOKS
Minneapolis, Minnesota

The little red hen had a full house.

She lived with a cat, a dog,
and a mouse.

The cat, the dog, and the mouse were a lazy bunch.

They slept all day while the little red hen worked.

She did all of the cooking, cleaning, and gardening.

One day, while she was in the garden, the little red hen found some grains of wheat.

PEAS

CARROTS

BEANS

11

"Who will help me plant this wheat?" she asked.

"Not I!" said the cat.
"Not I!" said the dog.
"Not I!" said the mouse.

"Then I guess I will do it myself," said the little red hen.

So she planted the wheat and helped it grow.

When the wheat was ready, the little red hen asked, "Who will help me cut this wheat?"

"Not I!" was all she heard.

"Then I guess I will do it myself!"
she exclaimed.

So the little red hen cut the
wheat herself.

After the wheat was cut, the little red hen said, "This wheat must be ground into flour. Who will take it to the mill?"

Again she heard, "Not I!"

"Then I guess I will do it myself," she sighed.

So the little red hen took the wheat to the mill. She returned with a big sack of flour.

"Who will help me make bread from this flour?"

"Not I!" shouted the cat.
"Not I!" shouted the dog.
"Not I!" shouted the mouse.

The little red hen muttered, "Then I guess I will do it myself."

She spent the entire afternoon baking bread.

When the bread was done, the little
red hen asked, "Who will help me eat
this bread?"

28

"I will!" yelled the cat.
"I will!" yelled the dog.
"I will!" yelled the mouse.

"No. I have done everything else myself.
I will eat this bread myself, too," the
little red hen said with a smile.

And she ate every last crumb all
by herself.

More *Read-it!* Readers

Bright pictures and fun stories help you practice your reading skills. Look for more books at your level.

Chicken Little

The Gingerbread Man

How Many Spots Does a Leopard Have?

How the Camel Got Its Hump

The Pied Piper

Stone Soup

On the Web

FactHound offers a safe, fun way to find Web sites related to this book. All of the sites on FactHound have been researched by our staff.

1. Visit *www.facthound.com*

2. Type in this special code: 1404809759

3. Click on the FETCH IT button.

Your trusty FactHound will fetch the best sites for you! A complete list of Read-it! Readers is available on our Web site: **www.picturewindowbooks.com**